It's not so easy being a princess. Or at least not for Merida, who would rather practise archery than learn to curtsey. To find out how this princess's one wish could change her kingdom forever, read along with me in your book. You will know it's time to turn the page when you hear this sound... Let's begin now.

Characters (in order of appearance)

Narrator	Nolan North
Merida	Kelly Macdonald
Queen Elinor	Emma Thompson
Lord MacGuffin	Kevin McKidd
King Fergus	Billy Connolly
Lord Dingwall	Robbie Coltrane

Text by Kitty Richards
Produced by Jeff Sheridan
Executive Producers: Randy Thornton and Ted Kryczko
Mastered by Jeff Sheridan at Soundworks, Burbank, CA

WALT DISNEY RECORDS

First published by Parragon in 2012
Parragon
Chartist House
15–17 Trim Street
Bath BA1 1HA, UK
www.parragon.com

ISBN 978-1-4075-9582-5

Printed in China

DISNEY · PIXAR

BRAVE

Bath · New York · Singapore · Hong Kong · Cologne · Delhi
Melbourne · Amsterdam · Johannesburg · Shenzhen

"Some say our destiny is tied to the land. As much a part of us as we are of it. But no one knows how we came to this land, or when. Only that there have been people here a long time, living in this land of mist and cloud, sun and rain, and snow. People who've come and gone, barely leaving traces they've been here at all. A fierce, proud land, filled with stories, and magic and danger."

A long time ago, there was a kingdom called DunBroch. The kingdom was ruled by King Fergus, who was strong and brave, and Queen Elinor, who was wise and fair. King Fergus had lost his leg in a fight with a demon bear named Mor'du. The king swore that one day he would defeat the bear once and for all.

The king and queen had four children. Hamish, Hubert and Harris were triplets. They were always causing mischief and yet they never got in trouble. And then there was Princess Merida. It seemed that she could do nothing *but* get in trouble.

Merida would be queen someday and her mother wanted to make sure that she was prepared. "A princess enjoys elegant pursuits. A princess laughs with her eyes. A princess *must* be knowledgeable about her kingdom."

A princess did *not* talk while chewing food. Or place her weapons on the dining table. Or even *have* weapons, in the queen's opinion. There were so many rules!

Merida much preferred to ride full-speed through the countryside on her horse, Angus. She loved archery and was very good at it. She liked to climb up waterfalls. And she liked to yell just as loud as she pleased.

One evening, Queen Elinor received messages from the clans of Macintosh, MacGuffin and Dingwall. She told Merida that the firstborn from each clan would compete in the palace games. The princess would marry the winner.

Merida was horrified. *Marriage?* "I won't go through with it! You can't make me!" She ran out of the room.

Queen Elinor followed Merida. She began a story about an
ancient kingdom whose king divided the land among his four
sons. But one prince wanted to rule the land himself. He followed
his own path and the kingdom fell apart.

Merida rolled her eyes. "That's a nice story."

The queen looked at her daughter. "It's not just a story, Merida.
Legends are lessons. They ring with truths."

Despite Merida's protests, the clans arrived. The princess was allowed to decide their challenge.

Merida had an idea. "I choose archery."

The queen threw her hands in the air. "Let the games begin!"

The clans competed in tug-of-war, hammer-throwing, cricket and finally, archery. Stocky Young MacGuffin tried his luck first, almost missing the target. And arrogant Young Macintosh's arrow was slightly off-centre. But to everyone's surprise, scrawny Wee Dingwall made a perfect shot!

Then a hooded figure stepped up. "I am Merida, firstborn descendant of clan DunBroch. And I'll be shooting for my own hand!"

Queen Elinor rose from her seat. "Merida! I forbid it!"

Merida began to aim. Bull's-eye! She hit the centre of every target.

Furious, Queen Elinor took Merida into the castle. "I've just about had enough of you, lass! You embarrassed them. You embarrassed me!"

Merida glared at her mother. "This whole marriage is what *you* want. Do you ever bother to ask what *I* want? I'm not going to be like you." Merida turned to the family tapestry hanging on the wall and slashed it with her sword. Then she ran out of the castle.

The princess raced through the woods on her horse. Suddenly, Angus stopped short. Merida flew off him and landed on the ground. She found herself inside a circle of stones, where glowing blue lights flickered. Merida followed the lights through the woods until she saw a small cottage.

When she opened the cottage door, she saw an old woman. Merida knew the woman was a Witch and she begged her for a spell.

The Witch sighed. She told Merida that long ago she had met a prince. He demanded she give him the strength of ten men.

"And did he get what he was after?"

The witch looked at Merida with narrowed eyes and nodded.

That was all Merida needed to know. "Then that's what I want. I want a spell that changes my mother. That will change my fate."

The Witch began throwing things into a cauldron. Suddenly, the concoction exploded. The Witch pulled out a dainty little cake.

When Merida returned to the castle, her mother was relieved to see her.
She hugged Merida. "I've been worried sick."

Merida was surprised "You were?"

"I didn't know where you had gone or when you'd come back. I didn't know
what to think. Of course, we both know a decision still has to be made."

Merida frowned. She showed Queen Elinor the cake. "It's a peace offering."

The queen smiled and took a bite. As the two walked down the hallway, the
queen stumbled. "Oh. Suddenly, I'm not so well."

Merida led Queen Elinor to her bedroom and tucked her
mother in. After a few minutes, the queen rose from the bed.
The sheet fell away from her and there, in front of Merida, stood
a – "B-B-B-B-B-Bear!"

Queen Elinor looked in the mirror and roared. What had the
spell done? What had *Merida* done?

The queen roared even louder and ran out the door.

Merida chased after her. "What are ya doing? Dad, the 'Bear King'? If he so much as sees you, you're dead."

Queen Elinor stopped. Merida was right. But they heard voices.

Panicked, they ran down the hallway and right into the triplets. With the boys' help, Merida guided the queen out of the castle.

Merida turned to her brothers. "Now, I'll be back soon. Go on and help yourself to anything ya want, as a reward."

The triplets were excited. They loved sweets!

Merida and Queen Elinor raced to the woods. They needed to reverse the spell, but night had fallen, so they took shelter. The next morning Merida used her bow and arrow to catch fish. Then she showed her mother how to catch them using her paws. For the first time in a while, Merida and her mother had fun together.

When they finally found the Witch's cottage, no one was there. Suddenly, a message came from the Witch's cauldron. It told them: *fate be changed, look inside, mend the bond torn by pride.*

Merida saw the same blue lights she had seen the day before.

She turned to her mother. "They'll show us the way." Merida followed the lights to a crumbling ruin. It was cold and eerie. "I have no idea what this place is."

Just then, the ground gave way underneath the princess. She tumbled into an ancient throne room.

There, she saw a huge stone sculpture of four princes. She looked up at her mother who was peering in from above. "You suppose this could have been the kingdom in that story you were tellin' me? The one with the princes?"

Suddenly, Merida noticed that the stone was broken before the fourth prince. She gasped. The prince in her mother's story and the one in the Witch's story were the same! "The spell. It's happened before."

Merida looked around. Claw marks were gouged in the walls. Bones were scattered about.

"Oh, no. The prince became ... Mor'du!"

Merida gasped as she turned and saw the evil bear behind her.

The princess barely escaped Mor'du. She and the queen ran through the woods.

Merida knew that they needed to reverse the spell soon. She remembered the voice from the cauldron. "Mum, if we don't hurry you might be a bear forever. Lest the outside become the inside. Like Mor'du. 'Mend the bond torn by pride...'. We have to get back to the castle. I know what to do. It's the tapestry."

At the castle, they found the clans in the middle of a huge battle.

Lord MacGuffin was angry. "You're the king! You decide which one of our sons your daughter will marry!"

King Fergus struggled to reach his throne. "None of your sons are fit to marry my daughter!"

Lord Dingwall didn't like that. "Then our alliance is *over*! This means *war*!"

Merida knew it was up to her to stop the fighting. It was her duty to choose who she would marry. She took a deep breath and faced the crowd. "Our clans were once enemies. But when invaders threatened us from the sea, you joined *together* to defend our lands. It was an alliance forged in bravery and friendship, and it lives to this day. And I know now that I need to amend my mistake and mend our bond. I've decided to do what's right."

But as Merida looked toward her mother, who was hidden,
she saw that the queen was shaking her head. She was telling
Merida that she didn't have to choose after all.

Merida looked back at the crowd. "And ... and ... break tradition? My mother, the queen, feels in her heart that we be free to write our own story, follow our hearts and find love in our own time."

The king put a hand on Merida's shoulder and smiled. "Just like yer mum."

As the crowd cheered, Merida slipped out and took her mother to the tapestry room. Suddenly, King Fergus threw open the door. He saw his daughter with a bear.

Merida had to protect her mother. "Mum! Run!"

As the queen raced out of the castle, the clans went after her. They didn't realize who she was. King Fergus locked Merida in the tapestry room to keep her safe, then rushed to join the group.

Merida had to get out. Her mother's life depended on it!

At that moment, the triplets appeared outside Merida's door. Only they looked a little different. They had finished off the spell cake and transformed into bear cubs! Quickly, the cubs helped their sister escape. Merida grabbed a needle, some thread and the tapestry. She frantically sewed the torn tapestry together as Angus galloped through the woods.

The hunting party caught the queen at the Ring of Stones.

Queen Elinor roared in terror as King Fergus walked up and raised his sword.

But Merida burst out of the woods and blocked the king. "I'll not let you kill my mother!"

Just then, a huge beast stepped into the Ring of Stones.

Merida gasped. "Mor'du!"

King Fergus looked up at the bear. "Kill it!"

But the demon bear swatted the hunters away like flies. He tossed King Fergus into the stones. Then he turned to Merida.

Queen Elinor roared and attacked Mor'du. The bears slashed at each other, but the queen fooled Mor'du into charging a broken stone. The stone toppled over, crushing the demon bear.

Merida looked at her mother. She had finished mending the
tapestry ... but the queen was still a bear. "I don't understand.
Oh, Mum, I'm sorry. This is all my fault. I want you back, Mum."

As Merida embraced her mother, morning light began to creep
in and fill the Ring of Stones.

Suddenly, Merida felt a human hand stroke her hair. Her mother wasn't a bear anymore! "Mum, you're fine!"

"Perfect." The queen smiled at her daughter.

The triplets came running over. They were boys again. All was right in the kingdom of DunBroch as the royal family hugged and laughed. Merida knew that from then on she could be a princess *and* still be herself.